FEET FIRST

AND OTHER SPORTS STORIES
Compiled by the Editors
of
Highlights for Children

Compilation copyright © 1995 by Highlights for Children, Inc.
Contents copyright by Highlights for Children, Inc.
Published by Highlights for Children, Inc.
P.O. Box 18201
Columbus, Ohio 43218-0201
Printed in the United States of America

ISBN 0-87534-644-8

Highlights is a registered trademark of Highlights for Children, Inc.

CONTENTS

FEET FIRST

By David Lubar

Jennifer got her first look at the Apalatchy River when the car went around the bend and pulled into the parking lot. Above the lot, a sign read, *APALATCHY RIVER GUIDES*. Jennifer wasn't looking at the sign; she was watching the water. It was big. This wasn't like the creek back home. This was big water—fast and fierce. It looked like it could swallow her up without even noticing.

"Let's go," her sister, Chris, said, running toward the small building at the back of the parking lot.

Jennifer walked after her sister, in no hurry to get into the river. Her parents followed.

"Can I help you with something?" the woman behind the counter asked.

"We're the Noonans," Chris said. "We're signed up for a trip."

The woman glanced at a book on the counter, then smiled and said, "You sure are. It'll be a good one. She's raging today. Let's get you outfitted. I'm your guide. My name's Diane."

"You hear that?" Chris asked. "She's ragin' today."

"Great," Jennifer said, frowning at the thought of an angry river.

The woman took them to the back of the shop, where she gave them life vests and helmets. "You wear these at all times," she said. "That is an absolute, unbreakable law. Got it?"

"Got it," Chris said. Jennifer nodded. The girls had been around water enough to know you didn't take it lightly. Jennifer was a good swimmer, but all of her swimming had been done in pools. She'd never been close to a river this size.

Diane got everyone equipped, then took them out the back door. A stack of rafts leaned against the shop. A separate raft waited for them at the edge of the river. "Okay, this is pretty simple," Diane said, "but pay attention. The water gets rough, but nothing you can't handle. Use your paddle to help keep the raft straight. If it gets too difficult, just sit back and enjoy the ride. If, and this doesn't happen often, but if you fall out, don't fight the water. The river is stronger than you. Ride the current; trust your life jacket." She looked at them. "If you are in the fast water, put your feet up in front of you. Don't try to swim. Got it?"

They all nodded. Jennifer wished Diane would stop talking about bad things happening. Chris jumped into the raft, going to the front where she would get splashed the most. Jennifer waited as long as she could, then went to the back and grabbed a paddle. Diane untied the raft and jumped in. They were off. "Remember," she said, "don't fight the river. You'll lose."

For a minute, they drifted smoothly down the river. "Wow!" Jennifer said when they hit the first stretch of white water. She hadn't expected such a jolt. The raft splashed through the rapid, churning water. She got tossed and sprayed and bumped. It was scary, but it was also fun. "Chris!" she yelled, trying to sound brave, "this is great!" If this was as rough as it got, she could handle it.

Chris didn't hear her over the roar of the water. Diane looked back and grinned. "It gets better ahead," she shouted. "That was just a small taste."

If that's the case, I've had enough, Jennifer thought. They entered a calm stretch. Ahead, Jennifer heard a roar, soft at first, just a whisper, then growing louder. In front of them, the water raced through a narrow stretch of rocks, churning into a white froth. Jennifer felt her body growing tense. The raft hit the rapids hard. The front of the raft lurched up. Then the back whipped up quickly. Jennifer was flung straight into the air.

"Yow!" she shouted, as she went up. She fell. The raft had moved on. She hit the water hard, just past the rapids. The life jacket kept her from going under. The river was yanking her along toward another stretch of rapids. She got a glimpse of the raft. Everybody was looking back, shouting something.

For an instant, Jennifer was petrified. She just kept thinking, *What should I do?* She was about to roll onto her stomach and swim when she remembered what Diane had said. Feet first, she had told them. Don't fight the river. Jennifer's instincts said swim, but Diane had said float with your feet up. She knew she had to make a decision. To do nothing would be the worst mistake. She had to trust Diane. She stuck her feet out in front of her body and laid flat. Suddenly, she was in the middle of a torrent of water. She was bounced and tumbled wildly, but she kept her feet up in front of herself. Big rocks whipped by on either side.

Hold on, she thought, *it can't last much longer.* Twice something hit her feet hard, but she spun off and kept moving. Finally, the water lost its fury. She saw the raft ahead. She rolled over and swam, not believing it was over.

Diane held out a paddle and pulled Jennifer in. "You okay?" she asked.

Jennifer nodded. She was too out of breath to say anything.

"Do you want to go on?" her father asked.

"Sure." She was getting her breath back. She sat down in the middle of the raft.

"A lot of people would have panicked," Diane said. "You did the right thing. If you had tried to swim, it would have been your helmet hitting those rocks and not your feet."

"I guess I kept my head in more ways than one," Jennifer said, looking ahead for the next rapids. She knew she hadn't beaten the river—nobody could beat a river. But she had flowed with it. She had met the river and survived. Now she knew she could handle whatever the river had to offer.

No Better Feeling

By Laurie Lisa

"Are you playing?" Rob bounced the basketball on the dusty asphalt between his Reeboks.

"I'm supposed to babysit Leonard." Julie jiggled the handle of the stroller impatiently. Today, her mother had insisted that Julie watch Leonard, and Julie was angry. She needed to practice every day this summer if she wanted to make the sixth-grade basketball team.

"It looks like he's asleep. Why don't you park him under that tree?"

Julie squinted over to the tree at the edge of the court. It wasn't far away. Surely, she would hear Leonard when he awoke from his nap. She had, after all, walked to the park looking for a game.

"You don't really expect *her* to play with us, do you?" asked a tall boy.

Julie recognized the boy, Bart, as being a year ahead of her in school. He had some friends with him. It would be a good game.

"Wait until you see her play," Rob promised. He winked at Julie.

"I'll play," Julie said. She did have a life of her own, despite being stuck with a baby brother. She pushed the stroller to the tree, her hands itching in anticipation. She always felt like this before a game—excited and nervous.

"Show them what you've got," Rob whispered, as they positioned for the tip-off.

When the ball was tipped to her, Julie took off down the court, stopping, dribbling, then passing to Rob, who made a jump shot from the free-throw line. The other team took the ball out of bounds, then passed to the boy Julie guarded. He was not expecting her quick hands. Before he could grab the ball, she flipped it out of his reach for a quick steal. Then, she was heading for the basket, her long legs flashing in the light. Her layup hit the backboard at the perfect spot, and the ball dropped right into the waiting net. It didn't even touch the rim.

It was a close game. Julie was caught in the rhythm of the bouncing ball, the chase back and forth along the length of the court. The sun beat down on her shoulders, and her legs grew pleasantly tired, as they always did from a good workout. The last shot was hers. She could feel it as she paused at the top of the key, jumped up, taking aim at the same time. She released the ball into a perfect arc that found its way into the basket and scored the winning two points.

"You're all right," Bart said, shaking her hand.

"Thanks." Julie smiled at Rob. There was no better feeling than playing a good game. She almost suggested that they all go for a Coke before she remembered the stroller. How long had they played? From the look of the sun dipping down into the western sky, it had been quite awhile.

She ran to the stroller. Her mother must be wondering where she and Leonard had been all afternoon. They would have to rush home. But Leonard was not sleeping inside the carriage. His blanket was there, but not Leonard.

"Rob! Leonard's gone!"

"Maybe he went home?" Rob suggested.

"He's only two years old! We have to find him. You search the tennis courts, and I'll look around the swings," Julie said. She was already heading for the playground equipment.

Her legs, tired just minutes before, were running faster and harder than she thought possible. She searched the face of each swinging child, but Leonard was not one of them. She passed the sandbox, where children dug with shovels and pails. Still no Leonard. She did not want to think of little Leonard lost, with his stubby legs and yellow curls. She was thankful that the park had a fence, so he couldn't have gone into the street.

She was out of breath when she returned to the stroller. Rob was already there, shaking his head. Julie's skin felt cold, even though the day was warm. They looked at each other for just a second, then headed toward the pond. Neither one of them dared to say it aloud. What if Leonard had stumbled into the water?

"Leonard!" Julie called. She had never felt so nervous before, not even before the championship game last year. And she felt more than that. Her mother had trusted her to take care of Leonard, and she had only thought of him as a burden. She had wanted to play basketball instead of giving up one afternoon for him.

"There he is!" Rob pointed toward a small figure sitting by the bank of the pond.

Julie ran to the little boy and scooped him up in her arms. She was so relieved to find him safe that she did not mind that he was covered with mud. She kissed his tender cheek.

"Oh, Leonard," she whispered, "I'm so sorry."

Leonard smiled as if he were the happiest baby in the world.

"What are you going to tell your mom?" Rob asked. "Leonard is one big mess."

"The truth," Julie said. She would tell her mom everything. She had learned something today. Being a good basketball player was not everything. Being a good sister was even more important. There was no better feeling in the world, she thought, as she cradled Leonard in her arms.

LITTLE JOHNNY SHORT-STEP

By Mary Louise Friebele

John limped as fast as he could, but still he could not keep up. As the other boys left him behind, John got mad at them. He hated school; he hated the whole world. But when he had hurried on down the hall and into the library, he forgot all about his limp. Miss Woodside had a new baseball book waiting for him.

A few minutes later he sat alone at a table in the library. He opened the new book and turned the pages slowly, looking at the pictures of the great baseball players. The walls of the library seemed to stretch away. He did not hear the whispering of the other children. Instead he dreamed he was at the ballpark with the crowd cheering and shouting for him.

"Come on, John! Slam it!"

The bases were loaded as he swung his bat. Crack! Up, up, and out sailed the ball. Around the bases he raced and slid home just before he heard the hard smack of the ball in the catcher's mitt. Safe!

John rubbed his eyes and shook his head slowly. He could dream all day, but he would never, never be on a baseball team.

Someone came up behind him, and he covered the book quickly with his arms. He knew the kids in his class laughed at him because he loved baseball. They could not understand why a boy with a short leg would spend his time reading about a game he could never play.

They had laughed and called him "Little Johnny Short-Step."

"That looks like a good book. Can I see it?" said Bob Green, the captain of the high school baseball team. "Move over," he said, giving John a friendly push. "Wow, look at that guy jump to catch a fly!" Bob flipped the pages of the book. "Do you like baseball?"

"Yeah," Johnny answered in a low voice. He began to curl smaller and tighter inside, the way he always did when someone laughed at him. He wished he could crawl away into a hard, tight shell like a turtle and hide. Now Bob would laugh and call him "Little Johnny Short-Step."

Bob looked questioningly at John. "I remember you now," he said. "My little brother is in your class. You're the kid who knows everything about baseball. Why don't you come to practice some afternoon?" He grinned. "We aren't like the guys in this book, but you might like to watch."

John tried to say "thank you," but the words would not come. Shyly, he nodded his head.

"Good," Bob said. "See you." And he went out of the library.

John sat quietly while the tight ache eased into a wonderful feeling of surprise and happiness. He had never dared go watch the team practice because he was afraid they would laugh at him, too.

That afternoon, right after school, John limped out to the baseball field near the school building. He pulled himself up on a low fence at one side of the field.

When Bob jogged out to the mound to pitch, he noticed John sitting on the fence. He waved and grinned at John.

21

By the fourth afternoon John knew the name of every player who came out for practice. He knew how they pitched, how they batted, and how they ran. As soon as he climbed up on the fence, he forgot his limp. He forgot the kids at school who laughed at him. He even forgot to be quiet so no one would notice him. He forgot everything but the game.

"Feet first! Slide feet first!" he shouted at a new boy on the team.

John had forgotten where he was sitting. He bounced up and down as he yelled and slid right off the fence to the ground.

Bob happened to see him fall. "That's not a good place to sit," he called. "You'd better come sit on the bench with us."

John limped proudly by Bob's side and sat down on one end of the bench. Some of the team members grinned at him.

John tried hard to remember to be quiet, but the game was too exciting. "This batter hits it hard up the middle. You're playing in too close," he yelled at Bob in center field.

Bob moved back just in time to catch a fly ball.

The kids on the bench looked at John in surprise. "You really do know baseball, don't you?" one of them said.

When Bob came off the field, he grinned at John. "Stick around, kid," he said. "You'll make a player of me yet."

Every day after that John sat on the bench with the team. They realized that he knew some things about the game that they didn't know. If they were uncertain about a play, they asked John, and he nearly always knew the right answer. The boys talked to him about baseball, and they listened when he talked. They were his friends.

One day Bob said to him, "You can't just sit here on the bench and be lazy all your life. We need a bat boy. All right?"

"All right," John answered quickly. He ducked down and picked up one of the bats. He couldn't even let Bob see how happy he was.

John already knew so much about baseball that no one had to tell him what a bat boy was supposed to do. He quickly learned which bat each player liked best and had it ready for him. He kept all the bats as clean as new. When a batter threw down his bat as he started to run, John picked up the bat almost before it hit the ground.

The boys practiced harder and harder as the time for the first game drew near. One day after practice, John was picking up the last bat, when Bob called, "John, come here a minute."

John looked up. The whole team was standing in front of the bench. As John limped over and stood in front of them, they smiled.

"John," Bob said, "the guys and I thought you should have a uniform like ours to wear for the games. Here it is." One of the other boys pulled a big box from behind his back and handed it to John.

John hung onto the box with both hands. He was too happy to speak. He was the happiest boy in all the world. "Little Johnny Short-Step" had made the team. And this time, he wasn't dreaming!

THE RELAY TEAM

By Judy Cox

Natalie flung open her locker, sending the door crashing into the locker beside it. The door bounced back and slammed shut again.

"Natalie! Nat, wait!" Ann waved across the dressing room. Natalie looked up, unsmiling, and peeled off her blue swimsuit. She dropped it in a soggy heap on the cement floor. She toweled dry and pulled on her clothes. Shouts of laughter came from the showers where the rest of the Blue Dolphins rinsed off. Natalie yanked a comb through her tangled red hair.

"Nat!" Ann caught up. "I want to talk to you." Ann clutched a towel around her waist. A drip ran down her cheek. She wiped it dry.

"What's to talk about?" Natalie scooped her wet suit from the floor and threaded it through the combination lock on her locker door. The other girls spilled into the dressing room, laughing and talking. Natalie looked at Ann. "Okay. I'll meet you outside." She shoved her towel and comb into her already stuffed backpack.

"Natalie?" called a short blond girl. Natalie pushed past her, out of the crowded room.

The morning air was cool. Natalie pulled the hood of her sweat shirt over her damp hair. Ann came over, and they crossed the street to the school.

"Nat," said Ann, "Coach Ruiz is right. Maureen is faster than me in the butterfly. She should swim that leg of the medley relay."

Natalie frowned. "But it isn't fair! You, me, Lindsay, Jill. We've been swimming together since first grade. It won't be the same without you. Remember last year at the regional meet? We came in third. Pretty good, but we promised each other that this year we'd take first." Natalie shifted her backpack to the other shoulder. "Now some new girl moves in and bumps you just two weeks before regional!"

"Natalie?" called the short blonde again, giving a timid wave. Natalie and Ann turned to look. Natalie turned away.

"There's Maureen now," whispered Natalie, grabbing Ann's arm. "Come on. Let's go."

"You go on ahead," said Ann. "I'll see you later." Natalie glared but hurried off to class, leaving Ann behind.

The next morning, after warm-up laps, Coach Ruiz called the medley team together to practice their relay. At the sound of the buzzer, Lindsay led off, backstroking with the smooth, clean motion that comes from years of practice. She reached behind her for the wall, turned, and headed back.

When Lindsay touched the wall, Jill dove off the block. She skimmed through the pool, bobbing up, spitting water, bobbing down again, kicking like a frog. When Jill reached the far end, she made a flip turn and headed back. She grabbed the wall with both hands and Maureen went off the block, back arched in a perfect dive.

Maureen *was* fast, Natalie had to admit. Her butterfly stroke was strong and powerful, faster and less choppy than Ann's. With Maureen on the team, maybe they could win regional. Natalie tucked a loose strand of hair under her cap and pulled on her goggles as Maureen made the turn.

A split second before Maureen touched the wall, Natalie dove in. She swam freestyle, the anchor leg. She swam as hard as she could, determined to show the new girl that the Blue Dolphins were as good as anyone.

Natalie reached the far wall and made her flip turn, pushing off with her feet. She swam back. She touched the wall, stood up, and pinched the water off her nose. She pulled off her goggles and looked up at Coach Ruiz. He shook his head. "Natalie, what happened? You left before Maureen touched. If you do that at the meet, we'll be disqualified." Natalie reddened.

That afternoon Natalie walked home with Ann. "I'm going to quit the relay team," Natalie said. "I don't want to be on it without you. If Coach wants Maureen on his old team, he can have her. But not me!" She kicked a rock into the gutter.

Ann grabbed her arm. "Don't quit, Nat! What about regional? What about Lindsay and Jill?"

"Why should I stay on the team if you're not on it?" said Natalie. "We're friends."

Ann shook her head. "This isn't about friendship," she said. "It's about teamwork. Even though I'm not on the relay team, I'm still a Blue Dolphin. And what about Lindsay and Jill? If you quit, they can't compete. There isn't time to add someone new." Ann smiled at Natalie. "C'mon, Nat. They've worked hard. They deserve a chance at regional. You owe it to all of us."

The next morning Coach Ruiz asked Maureen and Natalie to run through their legs of the medley again. Natalie stepped up on the block as Maureen made the turn. She warmed up, shaking her arms and legs. Lindsay, Jill, and Ann watched. Concentrate, concentrate, she told herself. Maureen hit the wall and Natalie dove in.

Natalie glided, arrow-straight, feeling the rhythm. She wanted to swim fast, swim forever. She didn't think about winning or losing or Maureen or even Ann. Only the feel of the blue silky water as it slid past her body.

She made her turn and came down the home stretch. The end wall loomed before her and she stretched her hands out. She slapped the wall and stood up, gasping, surprised to be finished so soon.

Maureen leaned down to give Natalie a hand. Everyone was grinning, especially Ann.

"We'll do it," Ann said. She smiled at Natalie. "No one can beat this team now!"

Terry's New Shoes

By Marilyn Kratz

"I hope Grandpa likes these shoes I bought with the birthday money he sent me," said Terry to his mom, as he tied the laces on his new white sneakers. "I'm going to keep them clean as new until he comes this afternoon."

"I'm sure Grandpa will think you spent the money wisely," said Mom.

Terry went out to sit on the front steps and wait for Grandpa.

"Hi, Terry," called Suzy.

Terry looked up. He saw Suzy, grinning down at him from the branches of the tall elm tree next door.

"Come and see the old squirrel's nest I found," she said.

"I'll look at it tomorrow," he shouted to Suzy. "I don't want to get my new shoes dirty."

"Woof! Woof!" Terry's dog ran up to him.

"Hi, Shaggy," said Terry. "I can't wrestle right now. I don't want to scuff these shoes."

Shaggy sniffed the new shoes as Terry brushed a spot of dust from them.

"How about a chocolate ice-cream cone to cool you on this hot afternoon?" asked Mom, poking her head out the door.

"Sounds great," said Terry. "But could I have my ice cream in a dish? A cone might drip on my shoes."

After Terry finished his ice cream, Mom said, "Grandpa won't be here for at least another hour. Why don't you run over to the park? I'm sure your friends are playing street hockey there."

"Okay," said Terry. "I'll just watch."

Terry stayed on the sidewalk all the way to the park. His best friend Sean, the goalie, was in the net when Terry arrived.

"Hi, Terry," called Sean, pushing his glasses back up his sweaty nose. "You're just in time to see me stop Lisa's shot!"

"Or miss it," added Lisa, smiling confidently from the blue line.

Terry watched Sean warm up as Lisa started toward the net. Terry knew that Sean hardly ever stopped the puck, but he yelled encouragement. "Give it all you've got, Sean!"

Lisa swung hard at the puck, trying to put it between Sean's legs. But Sean crouched low and batted the puck halfway back to the center line. He was so surprised that he just stood there, open-mouthed.

"Good save, Sean!" Terry shouted.

Sean turned to Terry and grinned.

Pete reached the puck next. He wound up, but Joanie blocked it away.

Then Joanie controlled the puck and ran up the left side. Joanie passed to John. John was almost up to their goalie.

Terry grinned. He knew John had a good slapshot. Sean would have a chance to be the winning goalie, which was something he hardly ever did.

"John!" called someone. It was John's sister, Meg. "It's time for your appointment at the dentist."

"But—" John began.

"Mom said you must come right now," said Meg.

John dropped his stick. "See ya, guys," he grumbled and followed Meg.

33

"Who's going to play for John?" asked Sean. Terry could see the disappointment on Sean's face.

"Looks like we win by default," said Lisa.

"Not yet," declared Terry. "I'll come in for John, if it's okay with both teams."

"Sure. Go ahead," the others agreed.

Terry forgot about his new shoes as he stood at the center circle. He didn't care if someone else made the goal, just as long as Sean had his chance to win the game.

Terry's hands were sweating as the referee dropped the puck.

Jan won the face-off. Terry tried to steal it away and missed.

Terry took a deep breath. Jan got behind Terry and passed to the center. Terry flew down the blacktop, trying desperately to catch up. Out of the corner of his eye, he saw Lisa scoop up the puck and slap it toward Sean. Terry didn't stop to think about his new white shoes. He had to slide to reach the puck.

Through the cloud of gravel swirling around him, Terry heard his team cheering. Sean was jumping up and down by the net, yelling, "You did it! You blocked it! No goal!"

Terry laughed and ran toward the others. Then he saw Mom and Grandpa coming toward them.

Quickly, he glanced down at his new shoes. They were covered with skid marks from the blacktop. He began to pound them with his hands.

"Grandpa," he gasped, "I wanted you to see the shoes I bought with your birthday money before they got dirty."

Grandpa laughed. "I can't think of anything better-looking than shoes that got dirty playing street hockey," he said. "That was a terrific slide. I'm glad I got to see *that*."

Terry glanced at Sean, who was still jumping for joy. Then he hugged his grandfather.

"Thanks for the birthday money, Grandpa," he said. "I had a wonderful time getting my new shoes dirty."

What Are You Fishing For?

By David Lubar

Joey sat on the edge of the boat dock, watching his rod, waiting for a bite. After a few minutes, he picked up the rod, reeled in a couple of feet of line, then set the rod down again, propping it against his tackle box.

Sure is slow today, he thought. He hadn't had a bite all morning. Still, being outside fishing on a beautiful day like today beat sitting inside watching television. The heat of the sun felt wonderful on his face. He turned his head toward the sound of footsteps as a girl approached. She was carrying a rod, a tackle box, and a paper bag.

"Hi," Joey said, nodding as the girl set down her gear a few feet away.

"Hey." The girl nodded back. Like Joey, she was wearing jeans and a T-shirt. She had on sneakers without socks and a blue cap with the name "Stephanie" sewn in thread over the brim.

Joey watched as the girl took a glob of sticky pink stuff from the paper bag and placed it on her hook. "What are you fishing for?" he asked.

"Carp," she said, casting her line in the water.

"Oh really?" Joey said, snickering.

"Yeah. Hey, what's wrong with carp?"

There was no need to argue with her. "Nothing."

"No, tell me," the girl insisted.

"Carp are trash fish," Joey said. He'd never seen one, but he knew they were slimy and ugly. "My dad says they're just stupid, lazy bottom-feeders," Joey told her. "They aren't worth anything, they taste bad, and they ruin the lake for the rest of the fish. I'm fishing for bass. They're the best."

"Well, I like carp," the girl said. She took a sandwich from the bag. "They don't ruin the lake; they help control the weeds. People just say those bad things because they heard someone else say them. Besides, my dad told me bass are stupid."

Joey just shrugged. He was about to say something when he noticed his line twitch. It twitched again, then started to pull out steadily, bending the tip of his rod. "At last," he said, picking up the rod. He pulled back hard, setting the hook. "Wow!" he shouted, feeling a solid tug that was a lot stronger than he expected. It almost brought Joey out of his seat. *Oh man,* he thought, *this is some fish—this is a big one.* He held tightly with both hands as the rod was nearly yanked from his grip.

"Looks like a good one," the girl said, bringing her line out of the water so Joey wouldn't get tangled.

Joey just grunted. The fish was taking all his attention. He let it run. There wasn't much choice at first; the fish was far too strong to be reeled right in like a small, flopping sunfish. If he tugged too hard, his line would break. Bit by bit, using all of his skill, he brought the fish closer to the dock.

"There it is," the girl said, pointing to a spot a few feet in front of them. She smiled, then giggled.

Joey finally got it to the dock. The glare of the sun on the water kept him from seeing the fish. He reached down, knowing that this was the biggest bass he had ever caught. He reached down, thinking how proud he would be to show it to his dad. He reached down and suddenly felt disgusted.

"Nice carp," the girl said.

"Stupid carp." Joey lifted it from the water, using all his strength to hoist the large fish.

"What do you mean," the girl said. "That fish just gave you the best fight you've probably had all summer. You should have seen yourself huffing and puffing to reel it in. It gave you a lot of fun, as much fun as any bass. I'll bet you'll still remember that fish when you're a grandpa. And all you can say is 'Stupid carp'?"

"But . . ." Joey wasn't sure what to say. He looked at the carp, really looked at it. In a way, it was very pretty.

"Hey, you got one of those trashy-looking carp," a voice said.

Joey glanced toward the newcomer. The boy went on, saying, "Carp are almost as bad as bass. Now me, I only fish for trout. They're the best. Anything else is just not worth my time. Dad says bass are stupid. And he says carp taste bad and mess up the water."

"Well, I say this is a nice carp," Joey said, winking at the girl. "Can I try some of that bait you have?" he asked her. "I sure wouldn't mind catching a bigger one."

"Be my guest," she said, pushing the bag toward him. "Maybe I'll even try for bass, if you'll let me have one of those worms."

"Sure," Joey said. Then they both laughed.

"What's so funny?" the new boy asked.

"You'll find out," Joey said. At least, they hoped he would.

The Secret Code

By Gay Bell

"I don't want to take care of the equipment! I want to be on the field with the other guys!" Scott looked angrily at the coach of the Meadowbrook Tigers. The coach turned away.

Didn't Coach Hunter know there'd been other athletes who were deaf?

Luther Taylor had pitched eight years for the New York Giants, and he was deaf. Kenny Walker played defensive end for the Denver Broncos, and he was deaf.

Why wouldn't Coach Hunter give him a chance?

Scott *knew* he could run. He'd won the fifty and one-hundred-yard dash races ever since first grade.

But because he was deaf, Coach Hunter said he couldn't be on the football team. "You couldn't hear the quarterback call the signals," the coach explained.

"I wouldn't have to hear him!" Scott protested, speaking loudly and signing furiously. "I could read his lips."

Scott's voice got louder. "I read everyone's lips. I hardly miss anything—EVER!"

"You couldn't read the quarterback's lips when he's got his helmet on," Coach Hunter said. "His face mask would be in the way. I'm sorry, Scott, but a missed assignment can ruin a whole game."

Coach Hunter patted Scott on the shoulder. He told him he could be the team manager and take care of the gear.

Scott nodded and walked away. He didn't want Coach Hunter to see the tears in his eyes.

Grimly, he rubbed his toe in the dirt. There must be *some* way I can play. There must be *some* way I can get the signals.

If only the other kids on the team knew sign language, he thought. *I guess I could try to teach Jim to sign. He could give me the signals.*

Scott shook his head. That wouldn't work. Someone on the other team might know the sign, too. They'd figure out the next play.

Slowly, Scott walked over and picked up a helmet and a kicking tee. He put them in the gear bag. He sat down on the bench.

He sat there a long time.

Suddenly, as though it had been given to him, an idea popped into his head.

Scott jumped up. *I've got it*, he thought. I know how I can read the signals! If only I can convince Coach Hunter.

Scott could hardly wait.

Coach Hunter was walking out onto the field. "That's all for today, guys. Be here tomorrow. Four o'clock sharp."

The coach picked up his clipboard. Scott rushed to his side. "Coach Hunter! I've got a plan! I know how I can get the signals! I'll figure out a secret code of taps. Jim and I can learn it. He'll give me the signals for the plays!"

Coach Hunter looked puzzled.

Scott hurried to explain. "Jim could give me taps on my leg. The taps would mean the same as the numbers he called. The taps would tell me what I'd have to do on the next play. One tap for a block, two taps for a screen pass, three taps for a run off-tackle. And I could watch the ball and move on the snap."

Coach Hunter grabbed Scott's hand. "I believe your plan will work, son! But you'll have to get Jim to agree. He'll need to learn the code. Bob, too. The backup quarterback will have to learn the taps in case Jim gets hurt. Let's ask them right now."

Scott and Coach Hunter walked over to Jim and Bob. The coach told them the plan.

Three weeks later Scott was beginning to get butterflies.

He retied his shoelaces. He made sure his mouthpiece was in place.

The team from Bear Creek was big. The Bears would be tough. The Tigers would have to play their best if they expected to win.

Scott swallowed. Would the secret code work?

Jim and Bob and he had practiced hard. They'd learned the code so well it seemed as though they'd always used the taps—as though they'd always played football that way.

But would they remember them *today*—when they were playing a *real* game?

What if he missed a tap and fouled up a play?

Scott pulled down his helmet. He ran on the field.

Scott watched the referee. The referee blew his whistle. The game had begun!

One play followed another.

Scott sighed with relief. So far the code was working. He was getting the taps.

But the Tigers couldn't break loose.

At halftime the score was Bears 6, Tigers 0.

Coach Hunter talked to the team. "The Bears' line is big. We've got to go to the air—throw more passes in the second half."

But the pass plays didn't work. The Tigers couldn't score.

There were only five minutes left in the game.

Fourth down!

The Bears didn't make their yardage!

The Tigers got the ball.

The Tigers hurried to huddle. Jim called the signals out to the team. Scott felt the taps on his leg. One tap. Then three.

Scott's heart pounded. That meant he was going to carry the ball!

The center hiked the ball to Jim. Jim faked to his left, then gave Scott the ball.

Scott had room to run. The blockers had done their job.

Scott raced down the field. He got to the Bears' 30—the 20—the 15. He was to the 10!

The Bears' safety was in his way.

Scott got around him.

He made it to the 4—3—2—the 1.

He was at the goal line!

He was over! He'd made a touchdown.

The Tigers pounded Scott on the back.

The Tigers' kicker ran on the field and got into position.

His toe came up. The ball sailed through the air.

A sigh echoed through the crowd. The ball had missed the center-post. The score was tied. Tigers 6, Bears 6.

Two minutes to go.

Scott stood on the sidelines, watching the action on the field.

The Bears huddled.

The crowd rose in anticipation.

"Tigers! Tigers!

Hold that line!

Hold that line!"

Scott couldn't hear the roar of the crowd, but it didn't matter.

He felt great!

He'd proved to himself and the other guys his deafness wasn't going to stop him.

Win or lose today—

He'd won.

WATER
GAMES

By Lynn Hartsell

It was the worst day of Megan's life. She didn't make the swim team. Her brother, Mike, did.

"Never mind, honey," said her mother.

"Maybe next year," said her father.

"You can come watch the meets," said Mike, holding up his team T-shirt.

Megan ran to her room and buried her head in her pillow. She could swim as well as Mike—only not as fast! Just because she was shorter and thinner and younger—it wasn't fair she didn't make the team!

A week passed before Megan felt like going back to the pool. There was a new poster on the wall. SYNCHRONIZED SWIM LESSONS . . . ASK CINDY.

Cindy was on lifeguard duty. "Hi, Megan! We missed you! Are you going to come out for sync-swim lessons?"

"I don't know." Megan wasn't sure Mom would want to make another car trip every day.

Cindy seemed to read her thoughts. "We use the pool right after swim team practice, so you and Mike could come together."

"Is this synchronized swimming like in the Olympics?" Megan asked.

"Yep—same thing!" Cindy laughed. "Only we'll start with simple movements. You'll be good at it, Megan. You're a strong swimmer."

Megan looked down at her bare feet. "I didn't make the swim team."

"That doesn't matter," Cindy told her. "Synchronized swimming takes smoothness, grace, and working together—not speed. In August, we'll have a water show! It'll be fun!"

When she got home, Megan asked her mother about the lessons. "We'll learn all those tricks, like the ones we saw in the Olympics, Mom. There's special dives and different strokes and dance routines—all in the water!"

Mike was watching a ballgame on television, but he was listening, too. "Water dancing! Some sport!" Megan stuck her tongue out at him. Mike did like to tease!

On Monday morning, more and more girls kept arriving at the pool. Megan knew the pool was only big enough for a circle of twenty girls. Maybe she shouldn't even try!

When the swim team was finished, Cindy asked all the girls to line up on the edge. There were thirty of them! "First, we'll learn the entry dive. Face sideways—put your arms overhead, feet together, toes pointed, and go over into the water like half a cartwheel." Cindy showed them how.

Soon Megan was having so much fun, she couldn't even think about not trying. This wasn't the swim team—it was even better!

Mike still teased. "Synchronized swimming! Ha! You know what they do, Dad? They pretend they're porpoises or ballet dancers. Some sport!"

Megan fought back. "It's in the Olympics—so it's a sport! Just you try twirling upside down, underwater. Or swimming with your head up." She rubbed the back of her neck. "It takes a whole new set of muscles."

One evening, the whole family went over to the pool. Megan dove in sideways without a splash.

She came up into a stretch float, arched her back, and went down with her legs in ballet position. She folded to a pike, touched her toes, and pushed up from the bottom of the pool with a great swoosh. Mom and Dad clapped. Mike shrugged, "Big deal!"

Later, Megan saw him trying the porpoise routine. He came up sputtering and shaking his head. She tried to help. "First, work on your breathing, Mike."

"Skip it!" Mike was embarrassed. "Who wants to be a porpoise, anyway?"

When they went to get their clothes, Mike couldn't find his locker key. "I had it pinned to my suit—it must have fallen off!" There was a chill in the air, and he started shivering.

"Probably when you were trying those tricks," said his Dad. "It must be at the bottom of the pool."

"Dumb synchronized swimming!" grumped Mike. "I *hate* swimming underwater!"

"I'll go look for it, Mike," Megan told him. "I'm used to swimming around on the bottom with my eyes open!"

Dad went back out to the pool with her. Megan dove in about the place where Mike had been swimming. She was looking for the key, when suddenly, everything went dark. The pool lights had been turned off. She started to come up but found she wasn't sure which way to go.

Just when she thought she *had* to breathe, she heard her Dad yelling. "Lights! We need some light here! My daughter's underwater!" Megan followed the sound of his voice and came back up to the surface. She was very glad to breathe air!

The lights went on and in a few minutes Megan dove back down. This time a silvery gleam caught her eye, and she came up with Mike's key in her hand. Mike smiled.

"Thanks," he managed to say through his chattering teeth. "Guess porpoises have their use!"

The next day, Cindy announced the date of the water show. Two girls had dropped out and two others would be on vacation. "There are still six too many for the team," Cindy said. Megan gulped.

"But we can work on that," Cindy went on. "Some taller girls might like to learn "twin" routines, okay?" Six girls waved their hands in the air. "Great! Everybody else will be with the team!" Megan felt a surge of happiness. She'd made it!

The girls learned to form stars and circles in the water. They practiced going under, hands joined, and coming up with a large splash like the park fountain. The water show was a great success— half the town came to see the team perform!

Mike still teased that sync-swim wasn't a "real" sport, but Megan knew how hard the team worked.

"And next summer," she told him, "we'll compete in team meets—just like you racers and divers."

"Really?" Mike was impressed. "There are meets for synchronized?"

"Sure," Megan smiled. "We're not just performers! We are very specialized athletes! Our sport takes endurance and concentration and. . . ."

"Okay, okay," laughed Mike. "So we'll both be in the Olympics!"

HOME-RUN FEVER

By Ruth E. MacGregor

Ronny Davis knelt in the on-deck circle, waiting for his turn at bat. Maybe this time he'd get that home run he had been yearning for.

He knew he was lucky to have made the team his first year at Milton High. And he was proud of his play in the field. But he was a light hitter, and it worried him. Milton needed strong hitters to win the league title, and Coach Burton had already benched a couple of his weaker batters. So Ronny dreamed of line drives and home runs.

Whap! Dick Bradford really whacked one into right field. The ball bounced off the wall. Coach Burton waved Dick on, and he slid in at third base just a split second ahead of the ball.

Ronny walked to the edge of the batting box and waited for the signal. Coach Burton just gave a quick nod.

Ronny frowned at the scoreboard: Milton 2, Hilldale 3. It was the bottom of the sixth inning, and there was one out. Milton needed a run to tie up the score. Ronny rubbed dirt on his hands and glanced at third base. Dick grinned at him, looking tense and eager.

Ronny knew this was no time to be swinging for a long ball—too easy to strike out. Almost any grounder to the right side of the infield would bring Dick in to score. Ronny took a short grip on the bat and waited for the pitch. It was a curve. Ronny chopped at it, and it bounded toward second base. The throw to first was easy, and Ronny was out. But Dick scored, tying it up 3 and 3. Milton's next batter flied out.

Ronny hid his disappointment and worked harder than ever in the field. He made some good stops and leaped high in the air to snag a fly, bringing a cheer from the fans. But all the while, he was thinking about his next turn at bat.

The score was still tied up 3 and 3 in the last half of the ninth inning when Milton's team came up to bat.

Joe Leach, the first one up, let the first pitch go by for strike one. He swung at the next one, slamming a line drive into left field. He rounded first and scrambled for second, sliding in safely just ahead of the throw.

Dick was up next, and Ronny moved to the on-deck circle. Dick chopped at the first pitch, and hit a roller toward first base. The first baseman outran him to the base, and Dick was out. But Joe had moved to third on the play.

Ronny walked to the plate, tingling with excitement. If Coach Burton would just give him the right signal, he'd swing away this time.

He saw Coach Burton again give that quick nod, and a half smile. Ronny caught his breath. He was free to swing away! He could try for a home run!

He took some time outside the batter's box, rubbing dirt on his hands. Something was bothering him. Coach Burton's nod meant Ronny was free to swing at the pitch if he wanted to. But it meant something else, too. It meant the coach was trusting him to do the right thing for the team. And the most important thing to the team right now was getting that winning run, not improving Ronny's batting statistics.

He stepped into the batter's box and shortened his grip on the bat. The ball whizzed close to his shirt, and he stepped back for ball one. The next pitch was the one he was waiting for. He bunted it on the ground with the bat, and it rolled slowly past the pitcher, between first and second bases. Hilldale's second baseman charged in wildly for the ball, scooped it up, and made the throw to the plate. But it was too late. Joe had scored and Milton had won! The Milton fans went wild.

Ronny was torn between the thrill of his team's winning and his own keen disappointment at not having had the chance to hit a long ball. His shoulders slumped as he walked toward the locker room. He suddenly felt very tired.

"Hey, Ronny! Ronny Davis!" It was Coach Burton, hurrying to catch up. Ronny waited.

The coach grinned and laid an arm across Ronny's shoulder. "Just wanted to let you know I'm proud of you. You came through in the pinch. A real team player! It's team players that win ballgames."

"Thanks Coach." Ronny straightened. Somehow he wasn't so tired now. *Someday,* he thought, *I might become a strong hitter.* He was surely going to try. But in the meantime he'd keep right on making Coach Burton proud—even if it meant scratchy little hits and dinky rollers instead of line drives and home runs. Milton needed strong hitters, but it needed team players, too. And Ronny Davis was going to be a team player, all the way.

Friends
for
Maria

By Margaret F. Keefauver

Maria's family had just moved from a tiny Mexican village to downtown San Antonio. Maria entered a school in the strange city. On the playground she saw many girls playing softball. She noticed at once that a girl named Edith was the star player on the team. Maria watched as the tall, sandy-haired girl gripped the bat and easily hit every ball far out into the field. Hesitantly, Maria asked Edith if she might play.

"We'll have to see how good you can hit first," Edith replied.

Maria could hardly hold the bat that Edith handed her. She swung hard at the first ball, even though it was over her head. Everyone laughed. Maria gripped the bat tighter and swung at the next two balls. She struck out.

"No use you trying to play with us," Edith yelled.

Maria walked home from school that day, lonesome and homesick.

One recess, Maria was standing on the sidelines watching a softball game, when a girl came up to her. Maria recognized her as the new girl who had entered her class that morning.

"Hello," the girl said cheerfully.

Maria was surprised at the girl's friendly manner. "Hello," she mumbled.

"What's your name?" the girl asked, tossing a ball up in the air. Maria noticed her ragged shirt and skinny arms.

"Maria."

"I'm Tina." She kept looking at Maria's dark face and eyes. Maria began to wish that the girl would go away.

"Where are you from?"

"Mexico. I've only been here two months." Maria lowered her head and kicked at a stone.

"Here, catch." Tina tossed the ball, but it bounced off Maria's fingers and dropped to the ground.

"Can't you catch a softball?" Tina asked in surprise.

"No," Maria said uneasily. "I tried to play soft-ball my first day at school. But I did everything wrong. Edith and the others laughed at me."

"They didn't mean anything," Tina said, grinning. "Don't feel so bad. I was as bad as you before I learned how to play. I can teach you."

"You will? Wow, that would be great."

Maria practiced hard every day. One afternoon Tina said, "Maria, don't you want to play with the girls tomorrow?"

Maria was silent. She was thinking of the times Edith had teased her. Maria picked up a bat and swung hard. She imagined her ball sailing far over Edith's head for a home run.

"I'll play tomorrow," she exclaimed. "I'll show Edith something."

At recess the next day Maria went up to Edith. "Which team can Tina and I be on?" she said in a determined voice. "We're going to play today."

Edith laughed. "So you really think you're good enough to play with us?"

"Sure," Maria answered stoutly.

"Well—okay," Edith said hesitantly. "We'll give you a chance."

In the outfield all the balls either rolled through Maria's legs or popped out of her hands, and at bat all she could hit were foul balls.

At last the game ended. "You didn't help us much," Edith said to Maria in a disgusted voice.

Maria sighed. She slumped down on the school steps beside Tina.

"I give up," Maria said dejectedly.

"You tried hard, anyway," Tina said. "Were you good at any sport in Mexico?" she asked, after a few minutes of silence.

"I used to win all the foot races," Maria answered.

"Why don't you enter the race Saturday, then?"

"What race?" Maria looked up quickly.

"All the grades have races every year," Tina explained. "And Edith is the champ."

As soon as Maria heard Edith's name, she jumped up and said, "I'd better start training right away if I want to win that race."

Every day the rest of that week Maria ran back and forth to school. By Friday she felt that her speed and endurance were as good as ever.

"Today's my big day," Maria said excitedly Saturday morning as she and Tina walked toward the starting line.

"A lot of the girls are rooting for you," Tina said. "They're tired of seeing Edith win everything."

Maria got into position along the starting line. She dug her toes and fingers into the ground, ready to spring forward. Glancing down the tense line of runners, she saw Edith. "I've got to beat her," she muttered.

"GO!"

Edith and Maria streaked to the front together.

Maria lengthened her stride, but Edith pounded close behind her. Maria heard Edith's steady, even breathing.

Maria gritted her teeth. EDITH'S NOT GOING TO WIN THIS RACE. Maria tore around the track. She felt as if she had wings. Her legs sped faster and faster. When she glanced over her shoulder, Edith was far behind.

Maria heard the shouts of amazement as she swept over the finish line.

"You ran like a deer," Tina shouted.

All the girls congratulated Maria. Everybody was smiling and friendly.

"Hey, Maria," one girl yelled. "You're the fastest girl in the school."

Edith came up to her with a wide grin. "Maria, we want you on our softball team," she said.

Maria was bewildered at Edith's offer.

"The way you can run, you could make a home run out of a single," said Edith.

Everyone laughed. But Maria laughed hardest of them all as she started toward the softball diamond with Edith and the rest of the team.

A
WINNER'S
GOAL

By Valerie Green

Sam felt like a loser! He tried so many things at school, and yet he didn't feel he was very good at anything. On the other hand, his best friend, Jason, seemed to excel at everything.

Both boys were on the cross country track team, and every week Jason was always one of the top three runners. Sam usually finished in the last ten. Jason and Sam both played soccer on the school team and for the local soccer club. But Jason was always the highest goal scorer on both teams! In school work, too, Jason nearly always got A's in every subject.

Sam wished that he could be more like his friend. He tried hard not to be jealous, but it wasn't easy.

The day Sam visited his grandmother after school, she asked him why he seemed so down.

Sam thought about his answer for a moment. "I just wish I knew the secret of Jason's success, Grandma," he said. "He does everything well! There isn't anything he's bad at!"

Grandma laughed. "I'm sure there must be something he has trouble doing, Sam."

"No, he's good at everything!"

"And you wish you could be, too. Right, Sam?"

"Well, it would be nice. . . ."

"Yes, it must be nice to be good at everything you do. But you know, Sam, not many people are. One thing I do know, though. Everyone can be really good at something."

"What do you mean, Grandma?" asked Sam.

"Well, if you work hard at *one* thing and improve on it every single day, pretty soon you'll find you *are* good at it! *Really* good. But you must set a goal for yourself, and then keep working at it."

Sam nodded. "I guess you're right. But everything seems to come easy to some people—like Jason. But for me it's harder."

"Well, Sam, maybe you're trying to be good at everything all at once. Why don't you try concentrating on just one thing at a time and really working at it."

Sam thought about his grandmother's words all week. He decided to set himself a goal as she had suggested. He loved soccer and really wanted to be a better player and a higher goal scorer. Since that's what he wanted, that's what he would aim for.

He knew one of his failings at the game was his running. So Sam set about improving it. Every night he ran three times around the block, timing himself as he went. During recess at school, he ran eight times around the track. As a result, his position in cross country began to get better, and once he even came in ninth out of a hundred runners.

Three weeks later, the day of the biggest and most important soccer game of the season arrived. His team *had* to win in order to retain their place in the league.

Just before the game, the coach told them that Jason had the flu and wouldn't be playing. Everyone on the team looked upset. They knew that it would be almost impossible to win the game without Jason.

The coach looked directly at Sam. "I want you to play Jason's position today, Sam," he said. "Your running has improved so much that I'm sure you can do it for us and score the goals."

Sam couldn't believe what he was hearing. He knew all the other players were doubtful, but if the Coach had faith in him, he was determined to do his best.

The game was tough. Both teams were playing well and their abilities were about equal. At half time, there was still no score. The second half began in much the same way, but, with only ten minutes of the game left, Sam suddenly felt he had the advantage. He knew he was playing better than he had ever played. He *felt* it in his bones.

The mid-fielder made a beautiful pass to Sam and now he had a breakaway . . . straight up the middle. His feet suddenly had wings as they dribbled the ball up the field. He knew he wouldn't let his team down. He positioned the ball and took a shot.

It was a goal the soccer club would talk about for years to come. It was Sam's moment of glory. As his teammates hugged him with joy and the crowd roared its approval, Sam caught sight of his grandmother who was yelling as loudly as the rest. He gave her the thumbs-up sign and she returned it.

He had set himself a "goal" and, by working at it, he had become a winner. Next week he vowed he would start working harder at math until his grade was better. With the cheers still ringing in his ears long after the final whistle had blown, Sam told himself, *there's nothing you can't do if you work hard at it.*

Girls' Team Catcher

By P. A. Sacksteder

"You mean we have to have a boy on our team!"

Tom cringed at the chorus of girls' voices that greeted him as he walked onto the baseball field. It wasn't his idea to get stuck on a girls' team. But during his family's summer vacation here on Rainbow Island, near a girls' school, there were no boys and no boys' team.

"Now, girls," the coach said, turning to the wall of Rainbow School shirts. "Don't you believe in equal opportunity for boys, too?"

"The question is—can he play baseball?" asked a short girl with big owl-rimmed glasses. She looked about 12, Tom thought.

He stretched as tall as his 10 years would take him. "I was first-string catcher on our boys' team," he announced proudly.

"Those bunch of little twerps," said a voice behind him. Tom jerked his head around angrily, only he had to look up. The red-haired girl was a whole head taller. She smiled at him and added, "Why don't we make him our cheerleader instead?"

"Oh, Katie, don't pick on him," said another girl.

"Okay, that's enough of these pleasantries," Coach Jenson said. "Let's get to practicing. Are you at least going to give Tom a chance to make the team?"

The girls' voices buzzed around home plate for a few seconds, then, "Why not . . . okay . . . sure . . . only fair to give him a try" came the sounds from most of the 15 girls. All except Katie, striding on long legs toward the pitcher's mound.

"Okay, Tommy, are you ready?" she yelled, smacking the ball into her pitching glove.

"My name is Tom," he shouted back as he crouched behind the plate. "Just throw the ball."

The pitch came toward him much faster than he expected, and he almost dropped it. But he also noticed it was right over the plate. Not bad. Katie was better than the good pitchers in his midget league, but he wasn't about to tell her that.

"Keep it lower," he yelled, throwing the ball back, "Or someone is going to knock it over the fence." His pitching partner just slammed the ball into her glove and glared back at him.

As the summer went by, Tom began to enjoy playing on the Rainbow team. And nobody teased him anymore, except for Katie, who continued to call him either "Tommy" or "Twerp."

"Listen, Tommy," she would say sweetly to him as they walked to the field. "Try and put your shoulders out a little more. You make an awfully small target for me to throw at."

Or, "Please don't throw the ball back so hard. I'm just a weak girl."

Tom hardly ever said a word to her. But the two still made a good battery, and the team won ballgames. By the end of July, the Rainbow girls plus boy had an 18–5 record and were tied for first place.

Then one day, the coach waved a letter in front of the team. "Great news," she said. "We get to play the Jackson team in a playoff game on Sunday. We travel to the mainland and play at Grant Field."

All the girls cheered, but not Tom. Grant Field was in his hometown. *Wait till all the guys see me on a girls' team,* he thought.

He was right. When the Rainbow team walked onto Grant Field, his school friends were packed in a small group behind home plate. Tom put his catcher's mask on to hide his face.

"Hey, Tom honey," someone yelled. "Wish I had curly blond hair like that. Maybe I could make a girls' team, too."

Katie walked from the mound to home plate and took the ball from Tom. "Wake up, catcher," she said. "We can't play this game if you stand there in a daze." She turned to go, then added, "Don't listen to those idiots. They're just trying to bother you so their sisters can beat our team. They'll give up after a while."

But they didn't. Every time Tom walked from the dugout to take his place behind the plate, his old buddies zinged him with another cheer about his curly hair or cute shoes or neat swing. They succeeded—he made two errors.

Errors or not, his team still had a one-run lead in the last inning. There were two outs, but the tying run was on third base.

Tom walked halfway to the pitcher's mound and tossed the ball to Katie. "Keep your eye on that base runner," he told her.

She grinned. "Just watch out she doesn't score on you," she told him.

The very next pitch, the batter slid her hand down the bat and bunted the ball hard, trying to get it past the pitcher. But Katie grabbed it cleanly and threw it, hard as she could, toward Tom.

Tom saw the runner, the biggest girl on the other team, barreling down the third-base line right at him. He snatched the ball out of the air just as she rammed into him, but he tagged her and still held onto the ball. He sat down, gasping for air.

Katie came running toward him. "Great catch," she said, reaching to help him get up. "Don't know how you held onto the ball." Then she smiled. "Guess you're not such a little twerp after all."

Tom tossed her the ball. "And you're the best pitcher I've seen, boy or girl," he whispered. "But don't tell my old midget team that."

Katie grinned then, saying as the other girls came up, "All Tom needs now is a Rainbow School shirt." She turned to him, "Would you wear it, or would you be embarrassed wearing a girls' school shirt?"

Tom shook his head. "I'd be proud," he said.

"Good," Katie said, then added wickedly, "as long as he doesn't tell his friends he won the game all by himself."

THE WINNER

By Neva A. Bartel

Brick bent over the bench lacing up his ice skates. *Tonight,* he thought, *I'll be getting the cheers!* During The Squirt Hockey Season, Brick played defense for the Warriors and watched the center, Gary, slap the puck into the goaltender's net and heard the crowds cheer.

Tonight it would be different! Coach was letting him play center. He'd show Coach that he could make points too.

Brick heard his name over the loudspeaker. He took a few short running steps on the toe of his blades and raced to the center of the rink, stopping in a spray of ice. Gary skated up to him.

"How did you talk Coach into letting you play center?" Gary asked. "The Blizzards are good. Coach made a BIG mistake."

"Yea." said Brick. "We'll see." He headed for the face-off circle so the game could begin. With his blade close to the ice, Brick was ready to sweep the puck to a teammate, but the Blizzard center was faster; he slapped Brick's stick and hit the puck to his own teammate.

The Warriors chased the Blizzards down the ice, past the neutral zone and into the defending zone. Brick dropped to his knees to block a shot aimed at the net. Gary stuck out his stick and snaked the puck from the opponent. Brick raced to the left of the net to receive a pass from Gary, but Gary didn't pass. He rushed down the center of the rink, dodging players, dragging the puck toward the net. He was going too fast. In a flash, the puck was spinning across the ice. Brick and a Blizzard man rode the puck into the boards so hard they bounced back and landed on the ice.

Coach pulled all three forwards and sent in fresh players. Brick and Gary sat on the bench.

"We could have had a point, if you hadn't been such a hot dog," Brick said as he wiped his face on the towel.

"Knock it off, Brick. There wasn't anyone who could take a pass, not even you."

A loud cheer went up from the spectators, and the red light flashed on. The Blizzards had scored. Both Gary and Brick groaned. In hockey, the team that scores first usually wins the game.

Five minutes into the second period, Coach nodded for the front line to go back on the ice. The Warriors had the puck, but the Blizzards stole it. The teams went back and forth down the rink, blades flashing, skating at top speed. A Blizzard was off-side and the puck went to the face-off circle. Brick sent the puck to a Warrior the minute it hit the ice. His teammate passed the puck back to Brick, and he raced toward the goal. Brick was alone, five feet from the crease, with the Blizzards' best player guarding him. He shot a backward pass right into the blade of a Blizzard. Gary flew across the ice, intercepted a Blizzard pass, and slapped it to Brick. Brick tried to score, slamming the puck in the direction of the net. The goaltender stopped the puck, causing it to rebound. In a flash, Gary caught the puck and saw that the goaltender was out of position. He knocked the puck into the vacated net. The crowd roared. The score was tied! Thanks to Gary.

At the end of the second period, the Warriors were exhausted. They had only eleven players to rotate while the Blizzards had eighteen. Brick sat on the bench wondering how they could win the game. He skated over to the end of the bench and knelt down to talk to Coach.

"Gary can handle the center position better than I can," he whispered. "I want to go back to defense."

"Glad you thought of it," Coach answered. The third period had five minutes left; Brick and Gary were still benched. Finally, Coach nodded to them.

"Gary, you take the center; Brick, the defense," he said.

On the rink, Gary caught the puck and pushed off hard with his rear skate. He moved fast, dragging the puck before him. A Blizzard tried to snake the puck away, and in the shuffle Gary shoved the player.

Gary was penalized two minutes—all the time that was left in the game. Two minutes to play and two players on defense and only two forwards.

We can't win, thought Brick.

Brick was hovering near the blue line when the puck went wild, and he caught it in the curve of his blade. He paused a half a second, his eyes sweeping the rink, and then he hit the puck as hard and as crisp as he could. The crowd was on its feet as the puck raced over the ice and into the net. The red light was flashing, and the crowd was roaring. Brick raised his eyes toward the penalty box. Gary was yelling and swinging his stick over his head. Brick did a slow figure eight on the rink. The Warriors had won the Squirt Tournament, not him or Gary, but the team.

The High-Point Trophy

By Isobel Morin

Laura's arms churned furiously as she swam toward the end of the pool. She slapped the wall, leaned back, and took a couple of deep breaths before checking the scoreboard. Another first place— her third of the meet.

The Marlins' head coach, Ellen Pringle, smiled as she pulled Laura out of the water. "Way to go. We may win the championship, thanks to you. And you have a good chance to be the top individual scorer and get the high-point trophy."

Laura grabbed her towel and headed for the bleachers, where the swimmers waited between races. She stopped at the scorer's table to pick up her first-place ribbon and to take another look at the trophy that would be presented to the meet's highest-scoring swimmer.

Laura knew that Ridgewood's Sharon Lee had also won three events in this county championship meet. So Laura needed to help the Marlins' relay team finish ahead of Ridgewood in order to wrap up that trophy.

Laura lay down to rest under the Marlins' banner. She had her head propped on a rolled-up towel when her teammate Molly poked her with a bare toe. Laura grunted and rolled onto her stomach.

"It's hot in here," Molly said. "Let's go outside."

Laura shook her head. "Coach told us to stay inside between races."

"We have almost an hour before our relay is called," Molly said. "Come on, Laura. I have a headache. Maybe the fresh air will help."

Laura hesitated. She didn't want to disobey the coach, but it was hot and stuffy inside. She picked up her sweat suit and said, "Okay, but just for a few minutes."

The girls circled the building and trotted over to the parking lot. Molly scooped a handful of snow from the edge of the lot and tossed it at Laura, then scampered away. Laura chased Molly across the lot, patting snow into a ball as she ran. Suddenly she slipped on a patch of ice. Putting her hands out to break the fall, Laura landed in a heap between two parked cars.

Laura struggled to her feet, then winced as she felt a sharp pain in her wrist. "The relay!" she yelled. "I have to swim the relay!"

"I shouldn't have made you come outside," Molly said. Her eyes filled with tears.

"You didn't make me do anything," Laura said. "Let's go to the locker room. Maybe if I put some ice on it, it won't swell as much."

The ice helped, but the wrist was swollen when Laura went out to the pool. She had the sleeve of her sweat shirt pulled down as far as possible to hide the injury.

It was almost time for the final relay. Coach Pringle called the team over for instructions. "The score is very close, girls," she said. "We're only four points ahead of Ridgewood, so we need to place at least third in this next relay race to clinch the championship."

Laura stood behind the others, holding her hands behind her back. Her wrist was stiff and painful. It would take a real effort to pull her arm through the water. But if she didn't swim, she would lose the individual scoring trophy.

But what if she cost her team the championship by swimming poorly? What if she couldn't even finish her leg of the race? She tried to shake off the thought, but it wouldn't go away.

The alternate for the relay, Grace Malone, wasn't very fast, but she could swim well enough to finish third. Laura knew what she had to do.

"I hurt my wrist," she said to Coach Pringle. "Maybe Grace should swim in my place."

The coach shook her head. "Too bad you didn't tell me sooner. Grace left with her parents about 15 minutes ago. And everyone else has already swum four events."

Laura stared at the pool. "Maybe I can swim, Coach. It's only 50 meters. Please let me try."

The coach put her arm around Laura. "Let's have the trainer take a look."

The trainer carefully examined her wrist. He determined that the wrist was only slightly sprained. "We'll tape it for stability, and you could swim without doing any damage," he said. "But it will hurt. You should ask your Mom and Dad before you try to compete."

Laura's parents were worried, but they eventually allowed her to participate. Laura hurried to join her teammates at the poolside. She jogged in place to warm up and eyed Sharon Lee, who would be swimming last for Ridgewood.

The Marlins' first three swimmers built a slight lead. As Molly touched the wall, Laura flew from the starting block. Her wrist hurt as she began to swim, but she gritted her teeth and continued to stroke.

Laura could sense that she was falling behind the other swimmers. *It's no use,* she thought, *we'll probably finish last.* But she continued to work, putting her head down for one last drive toward the finish.

At last Laura touched the wall. She looked up and saw that Sharon Lee was already climbing from the pool. Obviously Ridgewood had won the race, so Sharon would be getting the trophy. Laura's wrist felt as if it was on fire. She shut her eyes and sighed.

Coach Pringle wrapped a towel around Laura and led her to the bleachers. "You held on for third, Laura. You did it."

The coach's words were a blur. Laura had done what? She'd wasted the lead her teammates had built, and she'd barely been able to finish the race. And she'd lost her chance to be the meet's top scorer.

But when she saw her teammates hugging each other and laughing, Laura realized that they'd won the championship anyway. Suddenly the sting of losing the relay wasn't quite so bad.

"How's the wrist?" asked Molly.

"It hurts," Laura said, hugging her teammates. "But it will heal. Sorry I couldn't hold that lead you gave me."

"That's okay. You still got us the championship," Molly said. "That took a lot of guts."

Laura touched her wrist gently and winced, then she smiled. "Thanks," she said. "I think it took more guts than brains."

HOLD THAT LINE!

By Robert Hurley

"Hike!"

The ball shot back to big Willy Hays, and he came charging straight at me. I tried to stand there and wait for him—but I couldn't. I hated to admit it, but I was afraid. Willy Hays was just too big for me. When I saw him charging my position, his legs going up and down like hammers, something in me said, "Get out of the way!" And I couldn't tackle him. I tried to make it seem that I had tried, but I guess I didn't fool anyone.

"You big sissy," said George March, our center. I was angry and I wanted to say something back at him, but I didn't dare. *Anyway*, I thought, *he's right. I am a sissy.*

And this was my big chance, too. I had always been on the second string. The coach had never let me play in a game before that was really important. But this time the first-string left tackle was sick, and the coach had said to me, "Okay, Eddie, go in there and show me what you've got. If you do a good job, maybe I'll put you on the first string!"

I looked down at the ground. I felt ashamed. Then we went into formation again. I squatted down and leaned forward on my outstretched arm. I braced my legs and dug in with my cleats.

"Hike!"

"This time I'm going to tackle him," I said to myself. "I'm going to stop him."

Willy Hays was going to carry the ball. He looked around for a minute for somebody to pass to, but there was no receiver. Then he decided to run. And he came at me! I gritted my teeth. He got bigger and bigger as he came on, and to me he seemed even bigger than he was. How could his legs go up and down so fast, and how could he kick his knees so high? Here he was!

I tried to tackle him—I really did. But again that certain something inside wouldn't let me do it. I didn't have the nerve. I was a coward. At the last minute I swerved aside and only caught part of his shoe as he went by. I noticed he was smiling. He knew I was scared, and he was enjoying it.

The half-time whistle blew then, and we all went to the dressing room. We sat down on benches, and the coach stood at the other end of the room under the window. He talked to us.

"You're not doing so well in this game," he said. I thought he looked straight at me. He went on, "The score is all right. We're leading by six points. But all they need is a touchdown and an extra point, and we've lost the game." Everybody was quiet.

Then George March spoke up. "Coach," he said, "It's Eddie here." He pointed at me. I felt myself shrinking back, trying to hide in my football uniform. "It's his fault," George went on. "He doesn't try to tackle Willy Hays. He's afraid of him. Every time Willy takes the ball, they pick up five yards or so. He'd make a touchdown on every play if we didn't stop him in the backfield."

The coach turned to me. "You'll have to do better, Eddie, or you'll never make the first string."

Then the halftime was over and we went back to the game. I was so ashamed I could have cried.

The game went pretty well for a long time. We had the ball through most of the third quarter and made another touchdown. Then in the last quarter, they made a touchdown and an extra point, so we led by only five points. One more touchdown and they'd win the game! For some reason, big Willy Hays hadn't been running at me very much. They'd been trying a lot of pass plays that hadn't been working too well.

Now in the last quarter, with time running out on them, Willy started to break through me. Again and again he ran at me, with those knees kicking up, and I could never stick it out. He always got through for five or six yards. I could see that time was in our favor, though. If we could hold them off the goal line just a little longer, time would be up and we would win.

Then suddenly there was only time for one more play. We went into a huddle. George March was the captain, and he talked to us as we crouched around him.

"Listen, you guys," he said. "All we have to do is hold them this one time, and we've won the game. Don't let them through!"

Then somebody said, "But they only have about three yards to go for a touchdown. If they try to go through Eddie, they'll win for sure."

George looked at me with disgust. "We just have to hope they don't try to run through him. If they do, we'll lose."

Then we went back into formation. The crowd was yelling, "Hold that line! Hold that line!"

"Hike!" There it was! The ball snapped back. It went straight to Willy Hays, and Willy Hays came straight at me. He was smiling again. He thought he was going to break through easily and win the game for his team!

I said to myself, "This is it! Now or never!" And I stood there. If I could have nailed my shoes to the ground, I would have done it. He got bigger and bigger and still I stood there. Here he was!

I threw myself at his legs and shut my eyes. I held onto his legs as long as I could, and the next thing I knew we were both on the ground. The game was over. He hadn't made it. He hadn't got through me.

I got up, amazed. I felt great. I had tackled big Willy Hays, and I had stopped him cold. We had won the game! Out of the corner of my eye, I saw George March look at me and smile.